# THE MUMMY MAKERS OF EGYPT

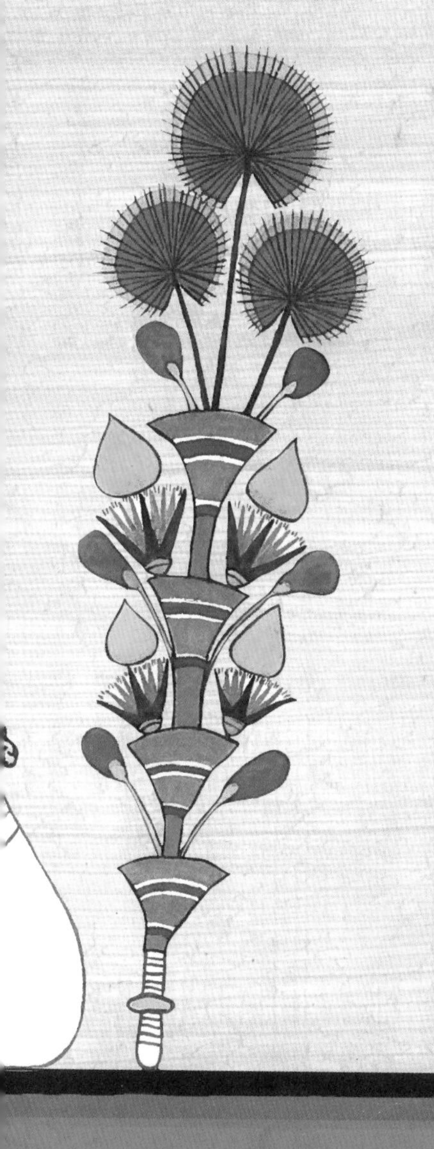

# THE MUMMY MAKERS OF EGYPT

TAMARA BOWER

NEW YORK • OAKLAND

THIS IS the story of the family of embalmers of the royal house, those who cared for the corpses and preserved them for eternity and were favored by the king. The head of the family, Paneb, whose title was "Overseer of Mysteries," served the royal house for twenty years. His first son, Ipy, had helped in the embalming house since he was very young, but now was to be formally trained.

The family lived in Thebes, the great capital of Egypt. Most people lived on the east bank of the Nile, the east being the side of the living. But the embalmers lived on the west bank of the Nile, in the City of the Dead, along with the other families who worked on the tombs and mortuary temples: mortuary priests, masons, sculptors, painters, and many others. In the morning Ipy went to school to learn to read and write, and in the afternoon Ipy went to the House of Embalming to learn by watching and to help with smaller tasks. Though Ipy had learned to read and write, he would never write down how the bodies were mummified; it was a secret passed down from father to son.

Embalmers were a class of priests; they were respected—most especially Ipy's family—for the high quality of their work. It is true that embalmers had to cope with strong odors while they worked. But they had smelled these odors all their lives, so they were used to them. And of course they bathed after work daily and used scented oils on their skin.

Embalming was a sacred art. An embalmed body ensured that one would survive into the afterlife. There were several aspects to the soul, including the ka, a person's double, which received the offerings at the tomb; the ba, a human-headed bird that could leave the tomb and visit the living; one's shadow, which could also leave the tomb and walk about; and the akh, the soul as a light reborn after death. All of these aspects of the soul were dependent upon the preserved body. However, if the body were to rot, the soul could fly to a statue of the deceased, and if the statue was destroyed, it could fly to a painting of the dead person, or it could even fly to his written name. But even so, one did everything one could to preserve the body as a home for one's souls.

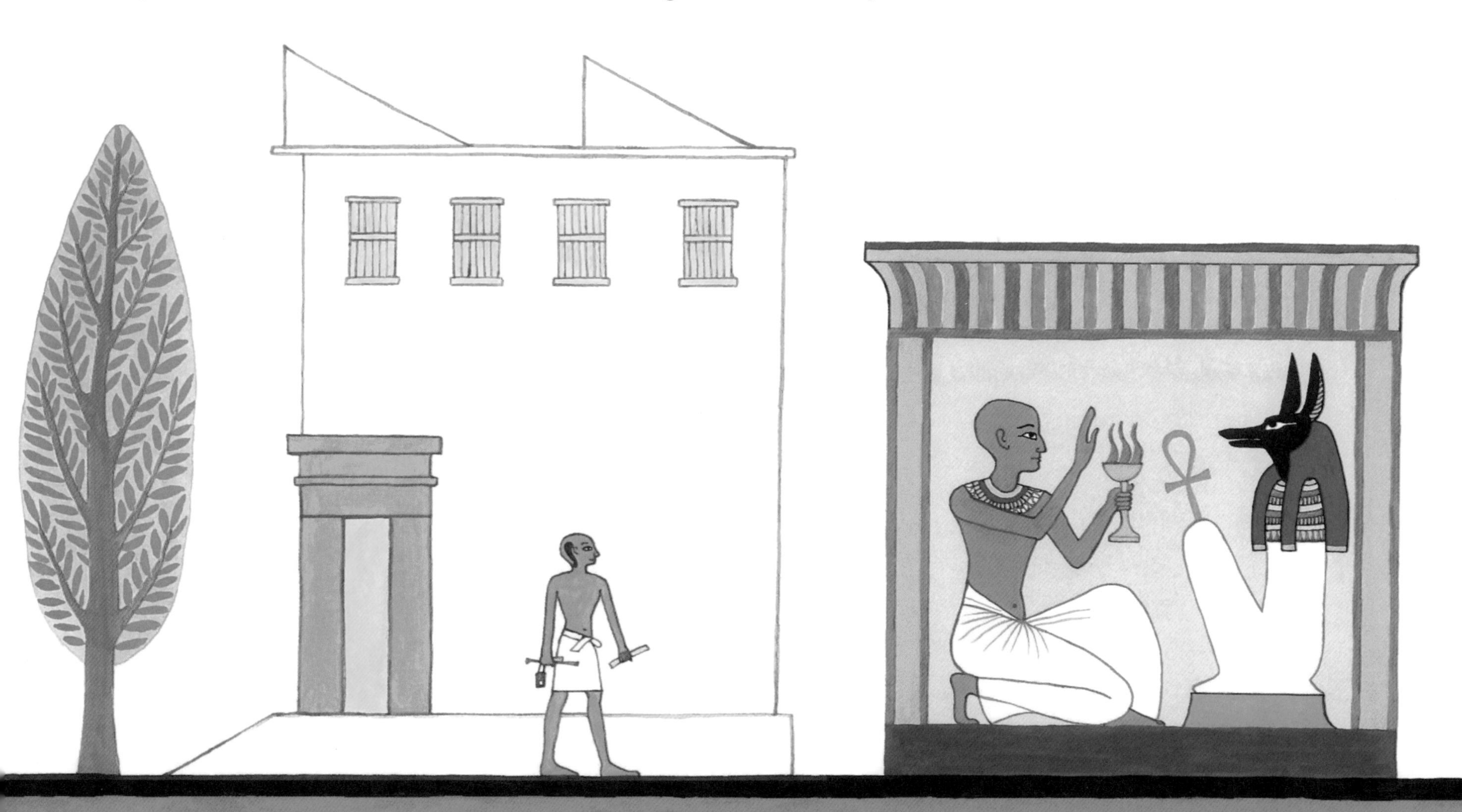

Upon death, the soul took a dangerous journey through darkness. A papyrus scroll of magical spells was placed with the mummy to help guide him through this journey and give him the correct answers for his encounters with many dangerous spirits and gods who would challenge him. He had to address each spirit and god by name:

**"I KNOW THEE, I KNOW THY NAME. DELIVER ME FROM THESE SERPENTS THAT ARE IN RO-SETU, WHO LIVE ON THE HEARTS OF MEN, AND WHO EAT THEIR BLOOD. FOR I KNOW YOUR NAMES: NASTI WHO LIVES ON HIS NEIGHBOR IS THE NAME OF ONE; HE WHOSE FACE IS TURNED AROUND IS THE NAME OF ANOTHER."**

The deceased arrived at the court of Osiris, god of the afterlife and judge of the dead. There his heart would be weighed against the feather of Maat, the goddess of truth and universal order. If the deceased's heart were as light as the feather, he would be welcomed into the Fields of the Blessed. If his heart was heavy with evil, his heart would be tossed to the monster Ammit, who would eat it, and he would perish. Rich and poor were judged, even the Pharaoh.

MAAT, GODDESS OF TRUTH — YUYA — THE FEATHER OF TRUTH — THE SCALE — YUYA'S HEART — THOTH, GOD OF WISDOM AS A BABOON — THE MONSTER AMMIT WAITING TO EAT THE HEART OF AN EVIL PERSON

"I AM NOT A DOER OF WRONG. I HAVE NOT TOLD LIES. I HAVE NOT CURSED. I HAVE NOT STOLEN. I HAVE NOT ROBBED. I AM NOT A MAN OF VIOLENCE. I HAVE NOT MURDERED. I HAVE NOT CAUSED ANYONE TO WEEP."

HORUS LEADING YUYA TO MEET OSIRIS

OFFERINGS OF LOTUS FLOWERS, FOOD, AND DRINK

OSIRIS ON HIS THRONE

NYPTHYS AND ISIS

Tradition tells us that Osiris was the first king of Egypt. He taught people how to farm. He also established government and laws. He was a wise and just ruler who brought prosperity to the Egyptians, who loved him. His brother Seth was jealous and killed him, cutting up Osiris's body and scattering the pieces all over Egypt. Osiris's wife, Isis, gathered the pieces and put them back together. In order for Osiris to be reborn as the god of the underworld, the jackal-headed god Anubis embalmed him so that Osiris became the first mummy. For this reason, Anubis was the Patron God of the Embalmers.

Ipy's father, Paneb, brought Ipy with him to the market to buy embalming supplies. The most important material was natron. Natron, a sacred salt-like substance from the Wadi Natrun area, was used to purify everything, and to dry the body and preserve it. They also needed oils, resins, and spices. Ipy's father usually went to the same merchants. He was a shrewd bargainer, and the merchants knew better than to try to cheat him. A few of the regular merchants had as their payment an agreement that Paneb would embalm the members of their family in exchange for a certain amount of supplies. Or sometimes Paneb would exchange other things for some of the supplies.

One day the embalmers were startled by a loud wailing. Obviously, the people were mourning someone important. Soon a messenger was asking for Paneb. He said, **"THE QUEEN'S FATHER, LORD YUYA, HAS LEFT THIS WORLD FOR THE WEST. MAY HIS SOUL BE WELCOMED TO THE LAND OF THE DEAD."**

In the palace, everyone was in mourning. In the town, businesses were shut, women were wailing and tearing their hair, the men stopped shaving and tore their clothes. Everyone put dust on their heads and faces, and beat their chests. A crowd wandered the streets, their heads covered in dirt, their clothes in tatters, singing funeral laments. No one ate. No one bathed.

The Egyptian people loved Queen Tiye. Her father, Lord Yuya, was a respected official in the court; he had many titles. Yuya had a good life. He was an old man when he died. He suffered the normal aches of old age—his teeth hurt from being worn down. He also had arthritis in his knees and back. This was common for an Egyptian of his age. But he died peacefully at home.

### YUYA'S TITLES

"Father to the King"

"The King's Lieutenant of Chariotry"

"Master of Horses"

"Priest of the God Min"

"Overseer of the Sacred Oxen of Min"

"The Lord of Akhmim"

"The Wise One"

"Favorite of the King"

Queen Tiye's mother Thuya's title was "Royal Ornament"—that is, a lady-in-waiting to the Queen Mother Mutemwiya. Thuya was very proud to be called "Royal Mother of the Great Wife of the King"—referring to her daughter, Queen Tiye. Thuya was also a songstress of the god Amun and of the goddess Hathor. Thuya and Yuya were not of royal blood, so it was a great and unusual honor that their daughter was chosen to marry Pharaoh Amenhotep III as his chief wife and queen.

**THUYA'S TITLES**

**"Royal Mother of the Queen"**

**"Royal Ornament to Queen Mutemwiya"**

**"Singer of the God Amun"**

**"Priestess of the God Amun"**

**"Dresser to the King"**

**"Priestess of the God Min"**

**"Favored of the Goddess Hathor"**

**"Favored of the Good God"**

On the west bank everyone burst into action. Yuya's death meant that there was much work to be done. Paneb immediately began giving orders to everyone who worked with him. The first thing was to set up the royal Tent of Purification. This was set up on a hill, where the breezes would clean the air. Poles set into the ground were spanned with linen. Mats covered the floor. There was an entrance on the western side and an exit on the eastern side. This symbolized the sun's journey through the underworld each night and its rebirth in the east every morning. So too would the mummy be reborn. Supplies were to be brought and everything arranged in order. Everyone who would be involved in the actual embalming of the body had to bathe, shave, put on clean linen clothing, and be ritually purified. Ipy's uncle, Bek, was left in charge, while Paneb went to accompany Yuya's corpse.

To embalm a body was an act of love and caring for the dead, and also a religious observation.

Yuya's body was put on a wooden bier and carried to a funeral barge, which brought Yuya's body across the Nile. Yuya's wife, Thuya, accompanied the body. She was in tears. Paneb stood proudly carrying his staff. When the boat landed, men carried Yuya's body in a procession to the Purification Tent. Then the mourners dispersed, and only they who would be embalming Yuya were left.

The body was laid upon a slanted table with runnels along the sides to allow the fluids to drain. First the body was washed with a solution of natron. This had an important ritual function, to purify the body spiritually as well as physically. A priest read prayers. The prayers recalled the birth of the sun from the waters at the beginning of time. So too would Yuya be reborn.

The next task was to extract the brain. Left in, the moisture would cause rot. Besides, the brain was not considered to be a very important part of the body. Extracting the brain took considerable skill. Paneb would be the only one to do this. Paneb stood on the right side of the body. He took a long, straight, sharp, and thick bronze shaft and gently inserted it into Yuya's left nostril. Then Paneb tapped the shaft until he broke the bone and pushed into the cranial cavity. Paneb took the straight shaft out and inserted another hooked tool

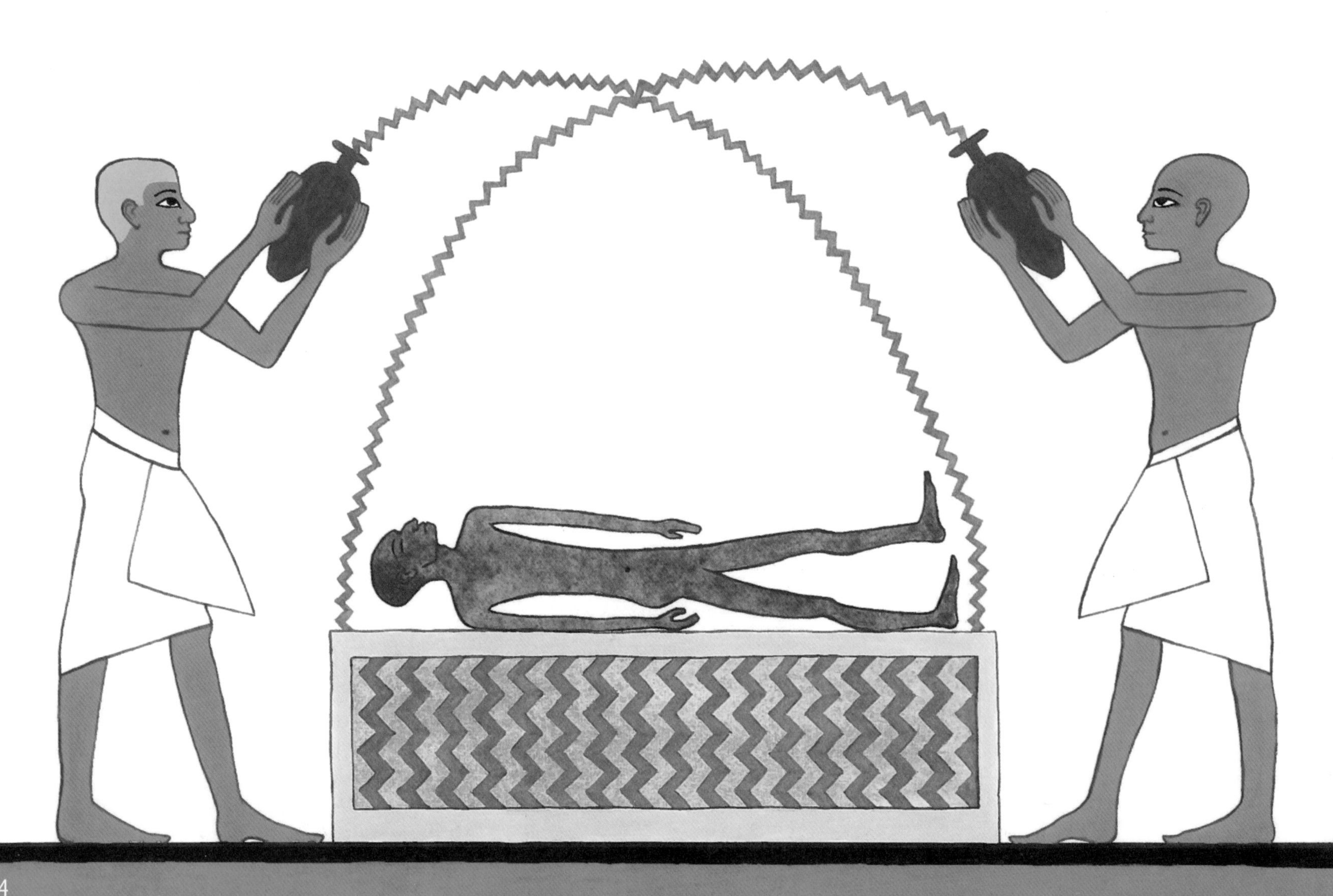

into the nostril. The hooked tool was stirred to break up the soft gray matter into liquid and was also used to pull out the more solid parts. The corpse was turned over so that the liquid could drain out of the nose. Then they poured palm wine into the nose to rinse it out and drained it again. Linen was then stuffed through the nose into the empty skull to help dry it up.

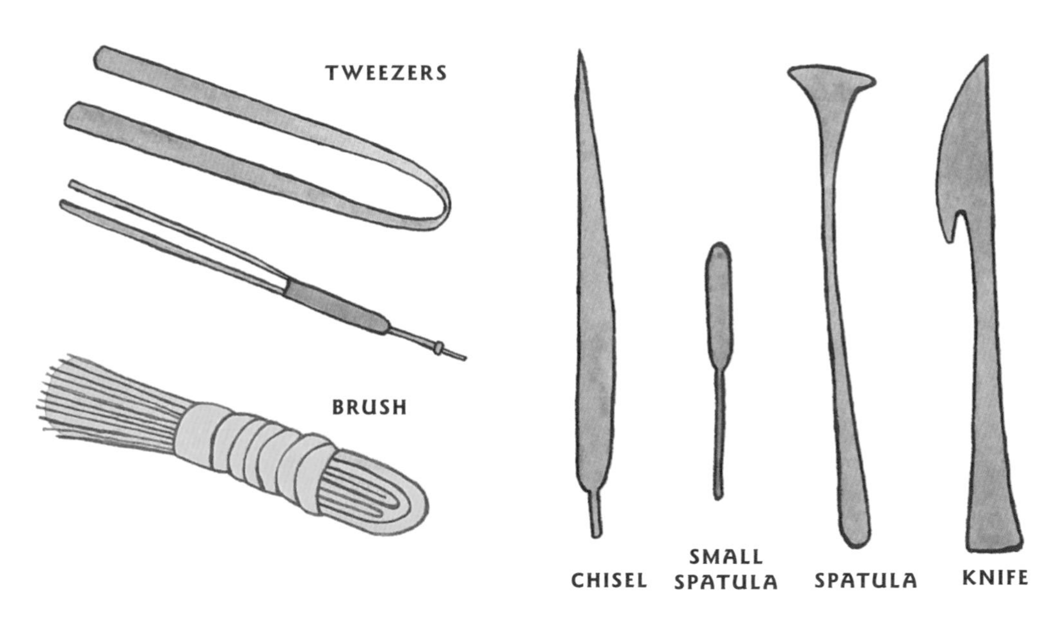


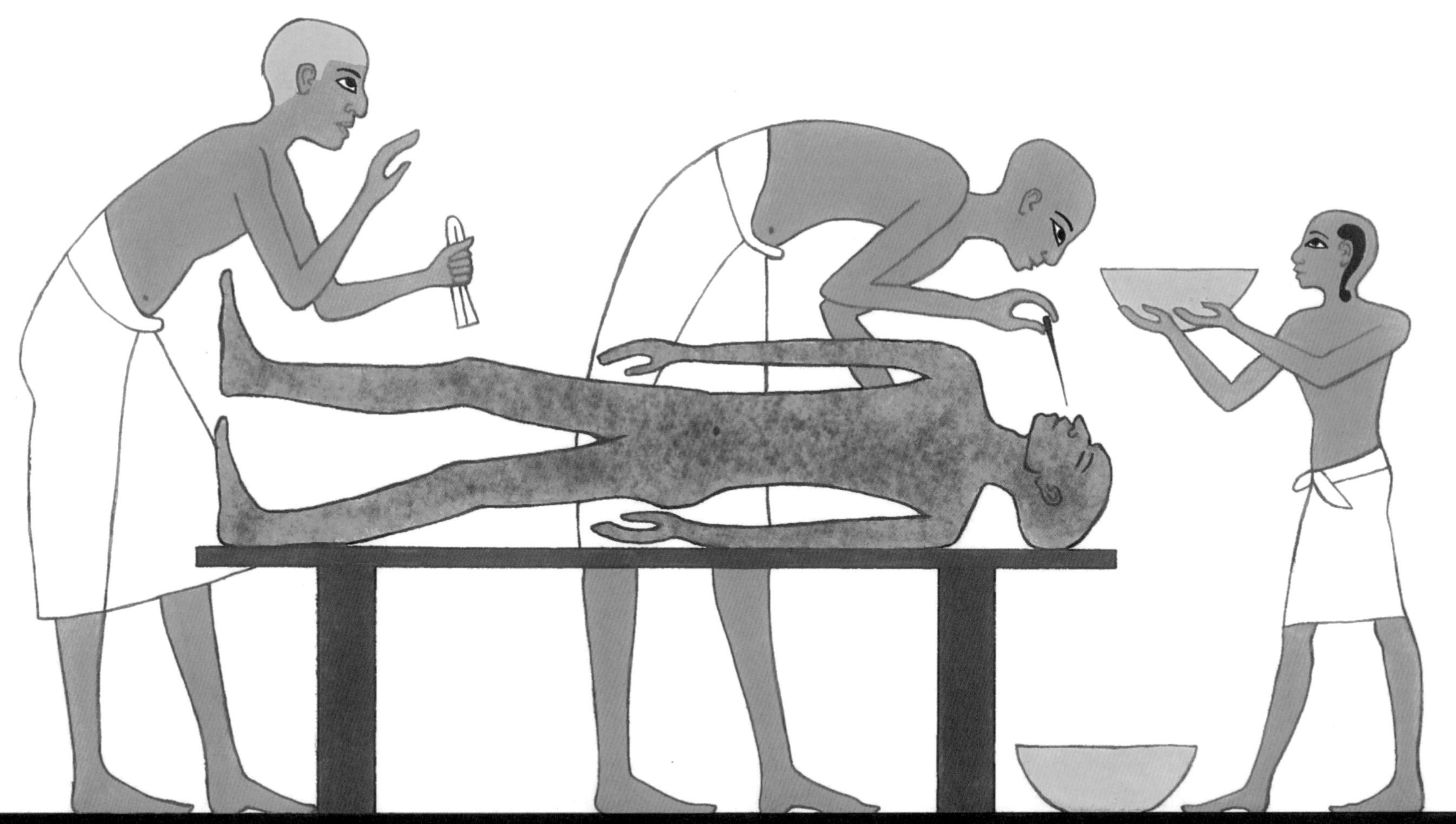

The next thing to do was to remove the internal organs. These also were very moist and would rot if they were not removed. Sabni, the scribe, marked on the left side of the abdomen where the cut would be made. Henuka was the cutter; it was his specialty to make the incision. First Henuka addressed the corpse of Yuya, asking forgiveness for what he was about to do. He had a very fine, sharp knife, made of Ethiopian stone. He made a cut along the mark that Sabni had made, just large enough for Paneb to be able to slip his hand in and pull the organs out. When Henuka had finished his work, the rest of the embalmers shouted insults and threw stones at him, for it is an abomination to cut open a body. This is a necessary evil. Henuka did a good job of making a clean cut, and they appreciated his skill. Henuka's coworkers were not really mad at him, but it was a necessary part of the ritual to pelt him with stones. He had learned to run fast, but Ipy got him good on his rear!

Paneb slowly slipped his hand into the cut and started to pull out the intestines. He explained to Ipy that this part had to be done by touch alone. The cut had to be small so as not to harm the body more than necessary, so one could not look inside. Then he guided Ipy to insert his hand and pull at the intestines. He pulled these out and handed them to an assistant, who rinsed them in a solution of natron. Then Paneb pulled out the spleen, the stomach, and the liver. As the liver is very large, Paneb had to use a knife to slice it into pieces to pull it out. As

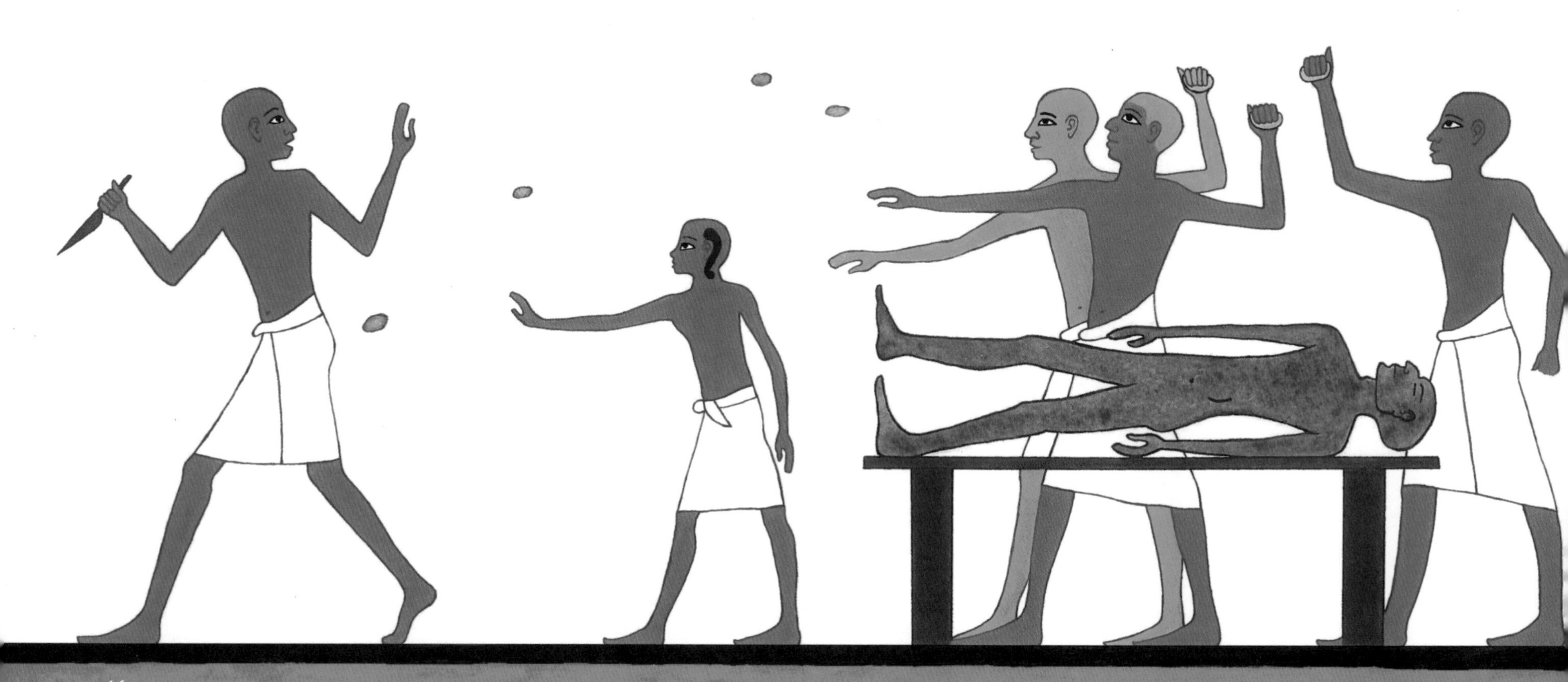

Paneb was careful, this took some time. He was also explaining how to do it to Ipy and having him try it now and again. Once Paneb got the abdominal cavity empty, he had to remove the lungs. He explained to Ipy how to use a knife to cut through the muscles and fibers of the diaphragm. He had to guide the knife through the incision and find where to cut by touch alone, using the fingers of one hand to guide him. Then Paneb plunged his whole arm up to pull out the lungs. Paneb explained to Ipy that it is very important not to disturb the heart while doing this. If for any reason the heart becomes loose, it must be put back in its place. The heart is the seat of intelligence and the house of the soul. For this reason it is left in the body. It is the most important organ, and great care is taken to protect it.

When Paneb was finished with removing the organs, his arms were covered with blood and fluids; assistants helped him and Ipy wash.

Other assistants took the organs, washed and dried each one, and placed them carefully in powdered natron. The inner cavity was rinsed with palm wine and then again with a solution of pounded spices. Assistants used wads of linen mounted on wood sticks to swab the inner recesses of the body. Then the outer body of Yuya was washed again, in water containing natron. Sachets of natron were inserted into the cavities of the body to help dry it out and to keep its shape.

**THE ORGANS WOULD be dried in natron and wrapped to look like small mummies. Then they were put into four human-headed jars. Called canopic jars, these would be placed in a box and accompany the mummy to the tomb.**

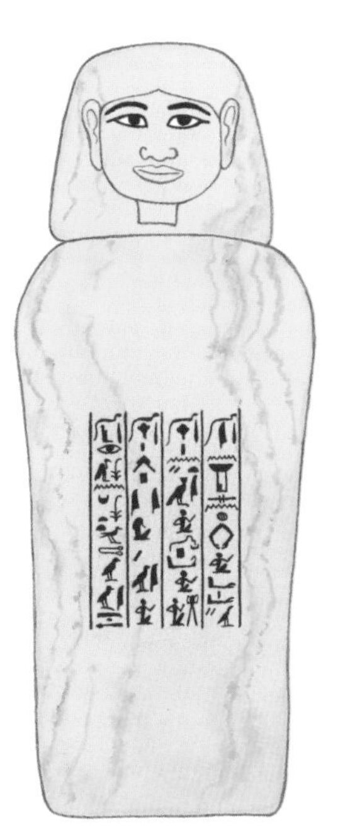

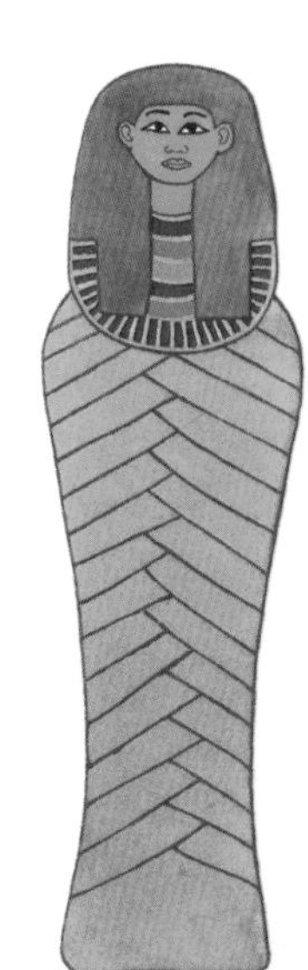

Although Yuya was not of royal blood, he was the father of the queen. Normally a noble's arms were laid straight down with his hands covering his genitals. But in Yuya's case they crossed his arms up on his chest, somewhat like a king's pose, to show his honored status.

Now was the time to cover the body in natron. The embalmers moved the body to another sloping table and carefully covered the corpse with powdery white natron. Quite a large amount of natron was used. The entire body had to be covered in dry natron from head to toe. As the body dried, water drained along channels carved out along the sides and into a basin at one end. The body had to stay in the natron for forty days. The natron had to be changed every few days as it soaked up the fluids, especially during the first twenty days.

The bodies were dried in natron outdoors, so that the sun would help with the drying. Care had to be taken so that wild dogs and jackals did not steal parts of the body. To animals, it was simply meat. Someone had to guard the drying bodies.

Strips of linen had to be prepared to wrap the mummy in. The resins, perfumed unguents, oils, and spices had to be gathered. There was also work to do on other mummies.

One of the tasks was to mummify food for Yuya's tomb. It was important to place in the tomb everything Yuya would need in the afterlife. High among the priorities was food. Chefs brought examples of Yuya's favorite foods. There were roast pigeons and barbecued ribs. These were placed in natron to dry them out. It was a simpler process to mummify food, as the meat had already been cleaned of the moist organs. The mummified food would be wrapped in linen bandages and placed in boxes to go into the tomb.

In forty days, when the corpse was dehydrated, it was taken out of the natron, and the bags of natron were taken out of the interior of the mummy. All of this, the bags and the natron, was placed in the jars with the other mummification waste materials, to be placed in the tomb.

They took the dried mummy to another part of the workshop, called the House of Beauty. That was where the finishing would take place, when the mummy would indeed become a thing of beauty.

They began at the House of Beauty by thoroughly washing the mummy again, both inside and out, and drying it with towels. It was important that the body be thoroughly dry before they started the bandaging, as any moisture would cause mold to grow.

The toe- and fingernails were dyed with henna. The body was rubbed with perfumed oil to soften the skin. The mummy was stiff and hard, and the oils helped to make the limbs a little bit flexible, to help with the wrapping. While massaging the oil into the dry skin, the body had to be turned carefully to avoid damage and so that none of the packing would fall out from inside. They used seven sacred oils. Jars of these oils were placed in the tomb also. All of these materials were very costly. When they were done massaging these oils onto the mummy, his skin was as soft as when he was alive.

Dry packets of linen and natron were put into the body cavities to help the body keep its shape. Hot resin was poured into the abdominal incision inside the body to protect the cavity. Then the incision was sealed with resin, and a gold plate covered it. They also poured resin into the nostril and into the skull, first with the head hanging back, then with the head horizontal, to ensure the entire cavity was covered. Then rolls of cloth were used to fill the nose and mouth to restore their shape.

The embalmers paused and all gazed at Yuya for a moment in pride and admiration. He looked as if alive. His personality showed on his stern but kind face.

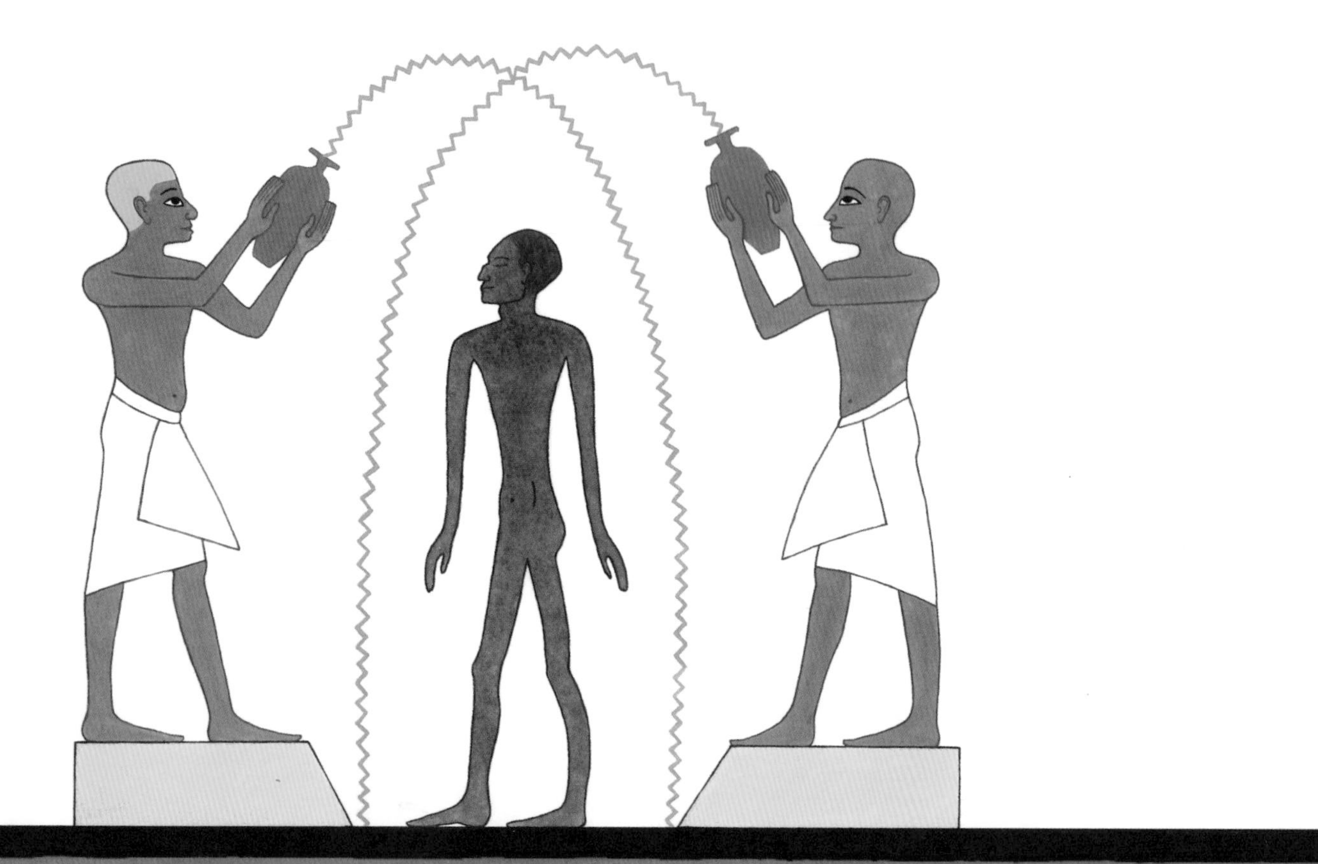

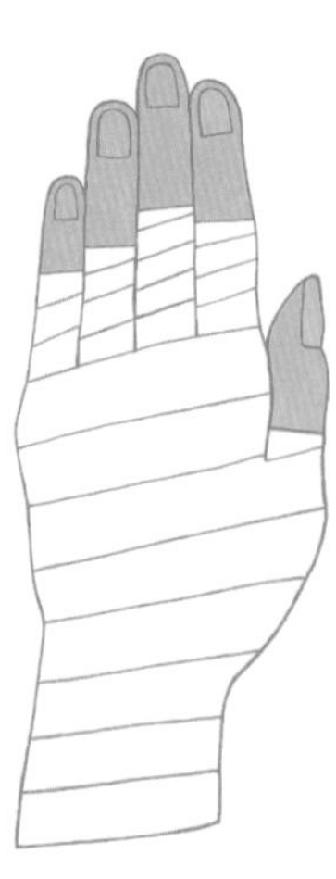

WRAPPED HAND WITH GOLD FINGER COVERS

Finally it was time to wrap the mummy in bandages. This also was an intricate and time-consuming process. It would take at least fifteen days. Amulets were put on the body. Then a layer of resin and bandages were applied. Then another set of amuletic jewelry was applied. The bandages were applied in a certain order, with appropriate spells chanted for each part.

Yards and yards of linens were used to wrap the body. Some of it was especially made for wrapping the mummy and some of it was made from the clothing of his family, as was traditional. And some of the cloth was inscribed with prayers from the Book of the Dead. The cloth was carefully arranged in rolls and neat piles according to size and purpose. The top of each pile was labeled. A scribe was responsible for keeping records of everything used, including the linen.

The head was first tied in place, with one band tied around the face holding the jaw closed, and another wrapped around the head and shoulders to steady the neck. On Yuya's throat was placed a djed pillar amulet, in gold—a symbol of Osiris and of stability. On the neck was the knot of Isis in red jasper. On the linen wrapped around the neck was written:

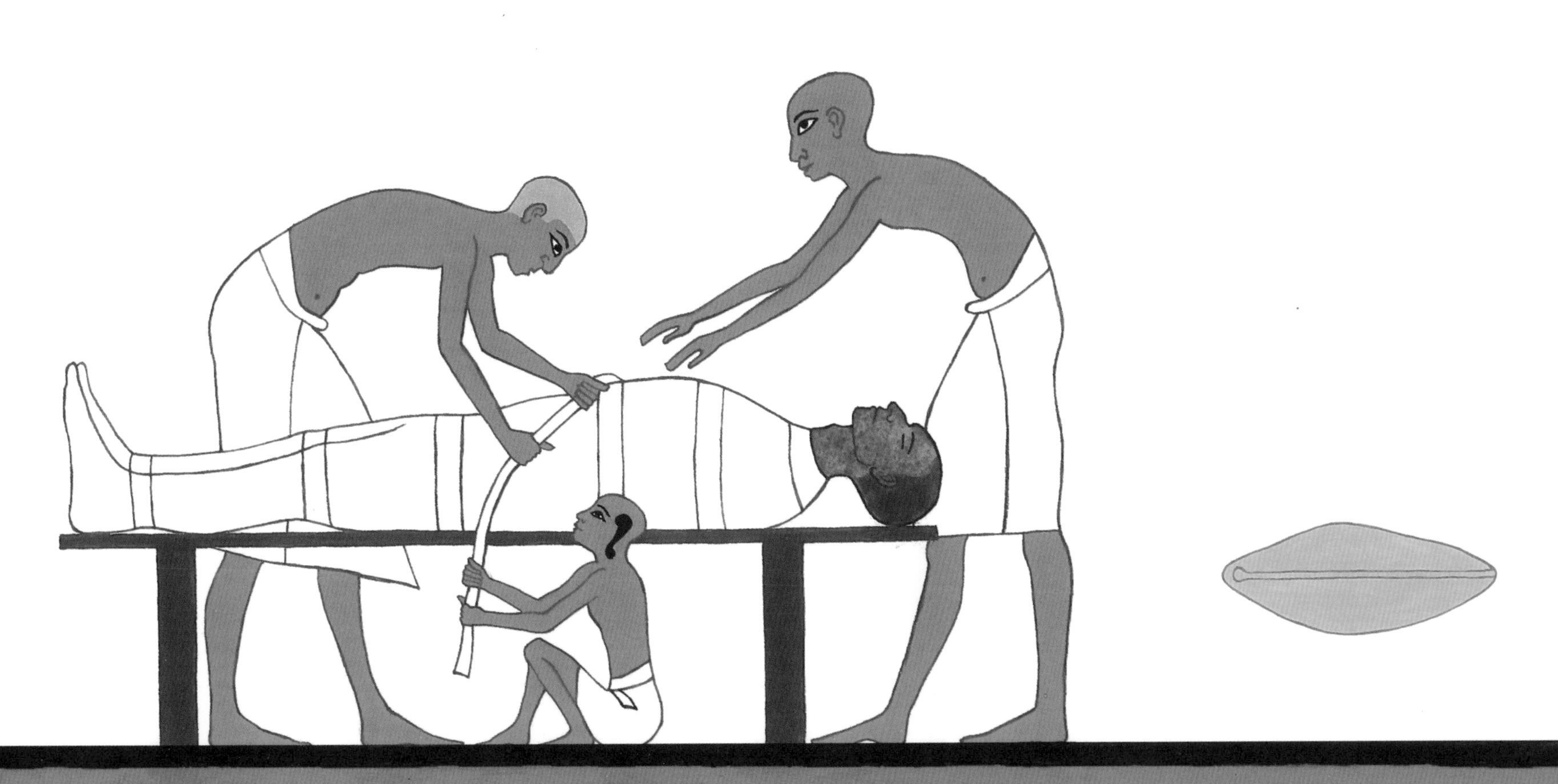

GOLD SEAL FOR ABDOMINAL CAVITY

**"THE BOOK OF BINDING WITH WORDS FOR THE MOUTH OF THOSE WHO ARE DELIVERED FROM DEATH; THEY ARE PUT ON THE NECK OF YUYA. THEY ARE NOT KNOWN BY COMMON PEOPLE. NO EYE HAS SEEN THEM, NO EAR HAS HEARD THEM."**

An amulet of a headrest in hematite stone was placed in the wrappings under the head. The lector priest intoned a spell:

**"O YUYA, MAY THEY AWAKEN YOUR HEAD AT THE HORIZON. RAISE YOURSELF, SO THAT YOU MAY BE TRIUMPHANT . . . YOUR HEAD SHALL NOT BE TAKEN FROM YOU AFTERWARD, YOUR HEAD SHALL NOT BE TAKEN FROM YOU FOREVER."**

Then they started winding narrow linen bandages around each finger and toe separately. Gold fingerstalls were placed over the bandages, which helped protect the fingers from breaking off. The arms and legs were bandaged next, each limb separately. And then the torso, with layers of wrappings and amulets. The bandages were wound in a spiral around the body. Each layer was brushed with melted resin, which protected the mummy by making it stronger, waterproof, and bug-proof. Then more layers of linen bandages were wrapped to hold the arms to the body and the legs together. Finally the whole body was wrapped in a shroud, which was tied onto the mummy with straps. The straps were cut from linen, covered with stucco, and gilded; the margins were painted green. The straps were firmly tied in the back.

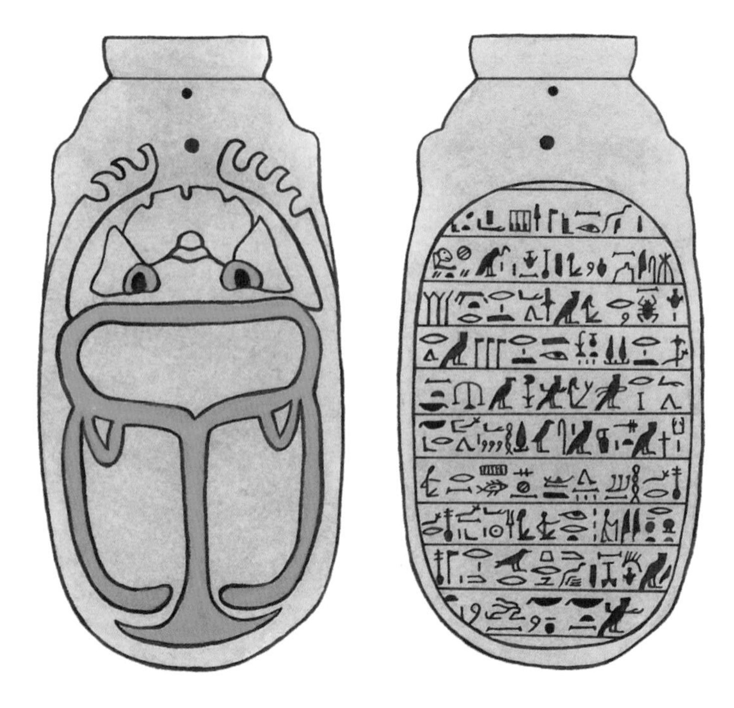

**THE GOLDSMITH was summoned, as many amulets had to be placed on the body and inserted into the bandages.**

**In a ceremony, the first pieces of jewelry were placed on the mummy. Rings were put on Yuya's fingers, bracelets on his arms, collars on his chest. Each of these showed his wealth and status, but they also carried magical and religious protection for his soul. The most important amulet was the heart scarab. It was very beautiful, a scarab beetle of jasper, encircled with gold. It was placed on Yuya's chest, over his heart. It was his heart, the seat of intelligence, that would be weighed against the feather of truth in the court of the gods.**

**"O my heart, which I had from my mother, O my heart, which I had upon earth, do not rise up against me as a witness in the presence of the Lord of Things; do not speak against me concerning what I have done, do not bring up against me anything I have done in the presence of the Great God, Lord of the West."**

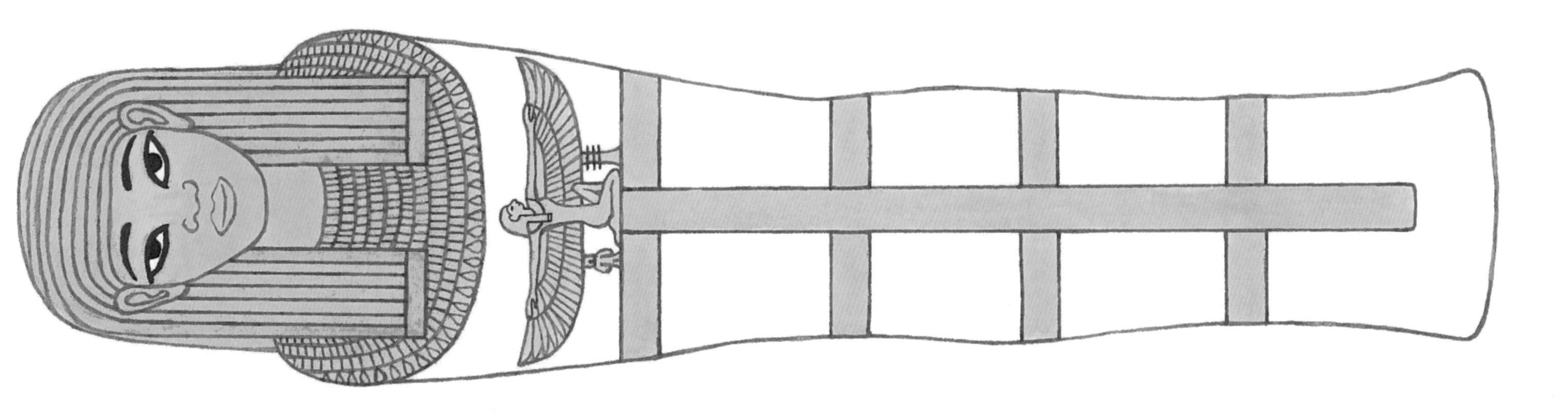

The last item to be placed upon the mummy was the gold mask. It was made of several layers of plaster and linen, and then gilt. The face was finely modeled. It was so beautiful. The eyes gazed out.

The embalmers had more to prepare for Yuya's mummy. The entire mummification chamber was swept clean and every bit put carefully into jars. All of the fluids and everything that touched the body were considered part of the mummy and could not be thrown out. It would be buried in Yuya's tomb.

Throughout the preparation of the mummy, priests were constantly reciting prayers for the soul of Yuya. Ipy's mother, Meryt, played the part of Isis. Ipy's aunt Tiaa played the part of Nephthys, Isis's loyal sister. They wailed and said magic words at the appropriate parts of the ritual. Ipy's father put on the mask of Anubis, the jackal-headed god of embalming, to personify the god.

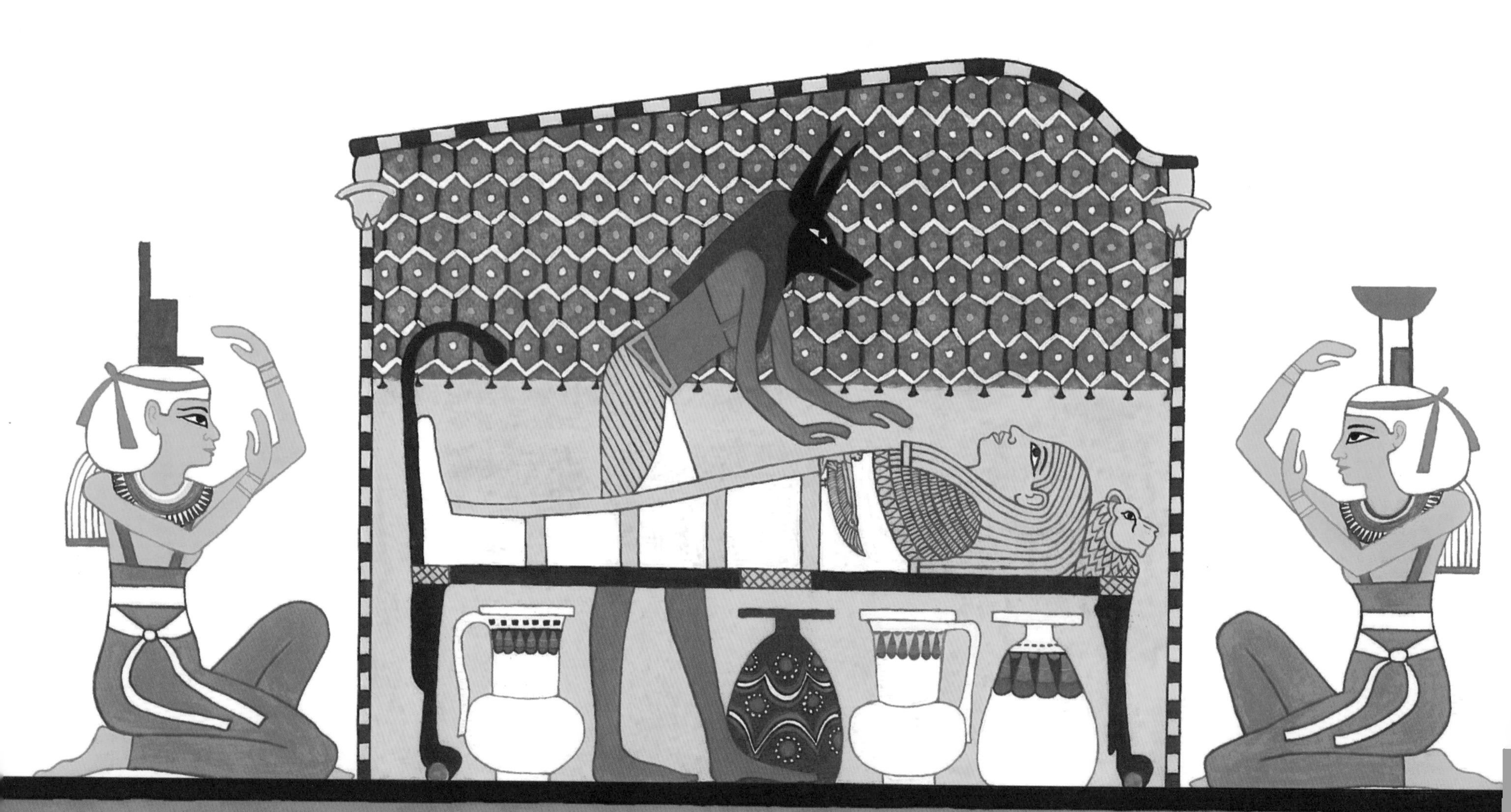

At this point the mourning family arrived: Yuya's wife, supported by their son, Aanen, high priest of Re at Thebes; Yuya's son-in-law, Pharaoh Amenhotep III; and Yuya's other son, Aye, who would become vizier and later a pharaoh himself. Also present were Yuya's granddaughter, Princess Sitamun; her brother, Prince Amenhotep IV; and his betrothed, Nefertiti. They too gazed upon the completed mummy with awe.

Yuya's grandson, Prince Amenhotep IV, would later become pharaoh and change his name to Akhenaten, bringing a revolution in religion to Egypt.

Now the final procession to the tomb began. Everything Yuya would need was brought to the tomb. The embalmers followed the procession to the tomb.

YUYA'S MUMMY IN THE COFFIN, IN THE SARCOPHAGUS PULLED ON A BOAT ON A SLED, WITH STATUES OF ISIS AND NEPTHYS

OXEN PULLING THE SLED

They moved slowly, praying and singing, to the Valley of the Kings, where *Yuya* would be buried in honor.

CHESTS, STAFF, AND SANDALS

CHAIRS, WRITING TOOLS, AND LOTUS FLOWERS

JARS ON STANDS

SHABTI MAGICAL FIGURES IN BOXES, SANDALS

PAPYRUS FLOWERS, POLES WITH HANGING BAGS AND JARS, THE MAN IN FRONT CARRIES AN INCENSE BURNER

At the entrance to the tomb, the mummy was raised to an upright position. Priests purified the mummy with water, while a lector priest chanted the sacred words. Yuya's eldest son, Aye, took the part of the sem priest and performed the important Opening of the Mouth ceremony. He raised an adze to the mummy's mouth, allowing the mummy to speak and eat in the afterlife. He also touched the mummy with other instruments, magically restoring all the senses of the body to the mummy: breathing, seeing, hearing, tasting, and touching. A calf was sacrificed and one of its forelegs offered to the mummy.

Years later, Aye would perform the Opening of the Mouth ceremony on the mummy of King Tutankhamen before becoming pharaoh himself.

The mummy was placed in a gold-covered coffin inlaid with semiprecious stones and glass. Strong men placed the lid on the coffin, and on the lid, an expertly carved face looked up with its eyes of obsidian. Thuya placed a wreath of flowers on the lid. That coffin was placed in another gilded wood coffin, which was placed in another, and finally carried into the tomb and placed in a wooden sarcophagus inlaid with gold.

A spot next to Yuya was reserved for his wife, Thuya, to join him when her time came.

ASSISTANT HOLDING BOWL AND FEATHER

LECTOR PRIEST HOLDING INCENSE BURNER AND VASE

FOOD OFFERINGS

AYE ACTING AS SEM PRIEST, HOLDING THE ADZE

TOOLS FOR RITUAL ON TABLE

When everything was placed in the tomb, everyone went back outside, and a priest in the role of the god Thoth swept the floor as they left so that no footprints would remain. Masons sealed the door, applying a layer of plaster and sealing it with the official necropolis seal. The tomb would be reopened eventually when Thuya joined Yuya in the afterlife.

FLOWERS THUYA MUMMY IN COFFIN PRIEST WEARING ANUBIS MASK FLOWERS TOMB ENTRANCE IN HILLSIDE

Outside the tomb, near the tomb entrance, was a feast. Meat from the slaughtered calf was eaten, as well as other food offerings. There was music and dancing. Yuya was on his journey to the afterlife, and his tomb was set for eternity. His body was safely preserved.

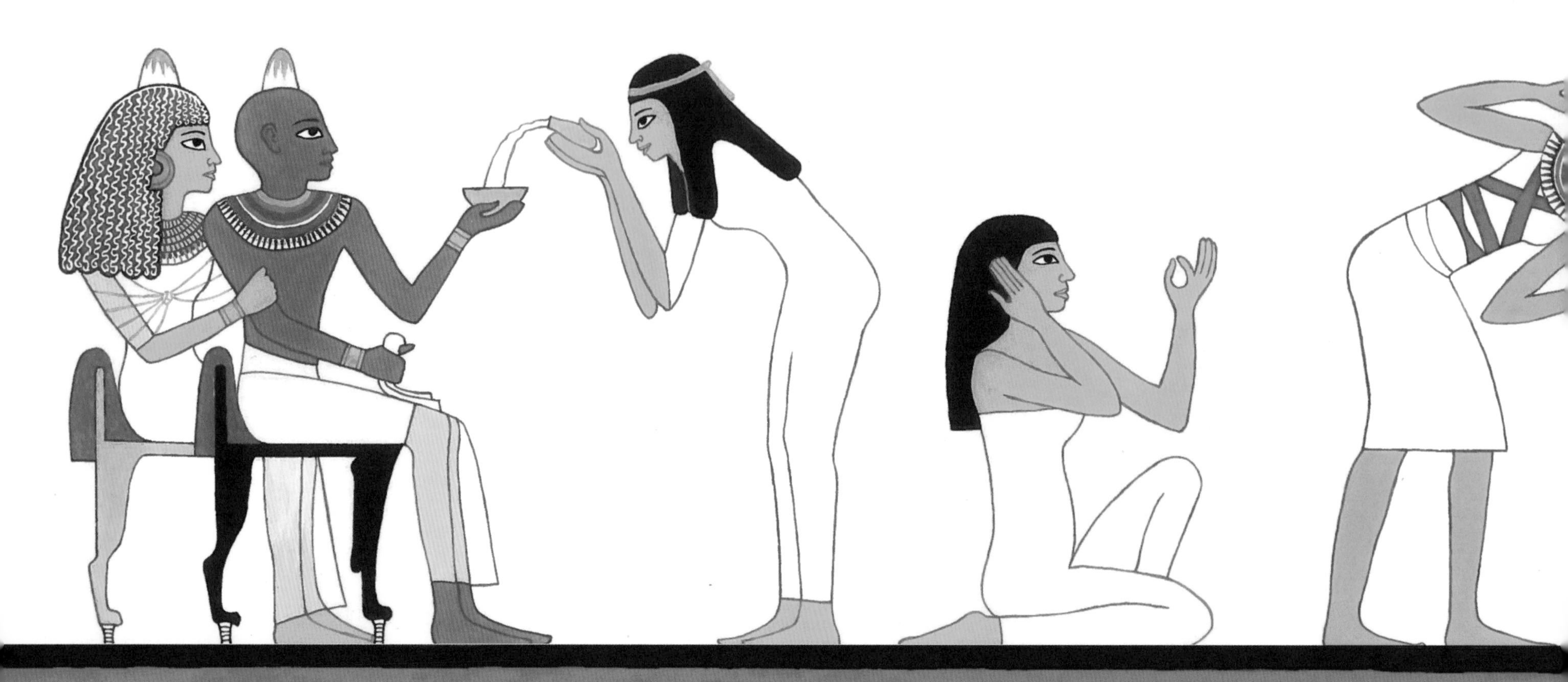

Yuya would be welcomed into the Fields of the Blessed, where he would enjoy all the best things in life. He would hunt, ride in his chariot, and eat his favorite food. His family would visit his offering chapel, bringing offerings of food and drink. They would say prayers for him and could even write him a letter. Every time someone remembers Yuya or says his name aloud, his soul is given life in the afterworld. And three thousand years later, he is still remembered.

"THIS BOOK IS FINISHED. IT IS AS IT WAS FOUND WRITTEN FROM BEGINNING TO END, HAVING BEEN WRITTEN OUT, CHECKED, EXAMINED, AND CORRECTED SIGN BY SIGN."

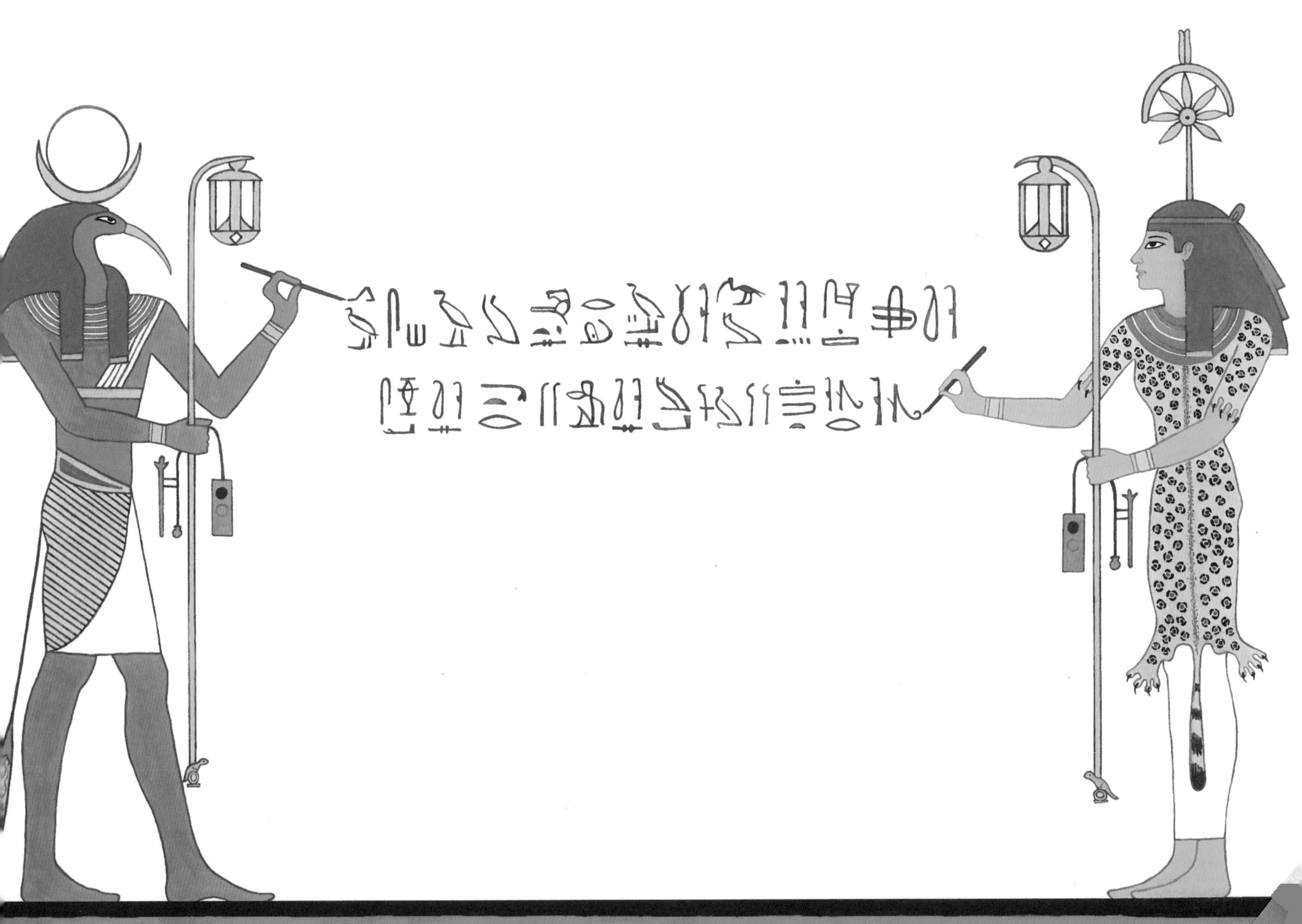

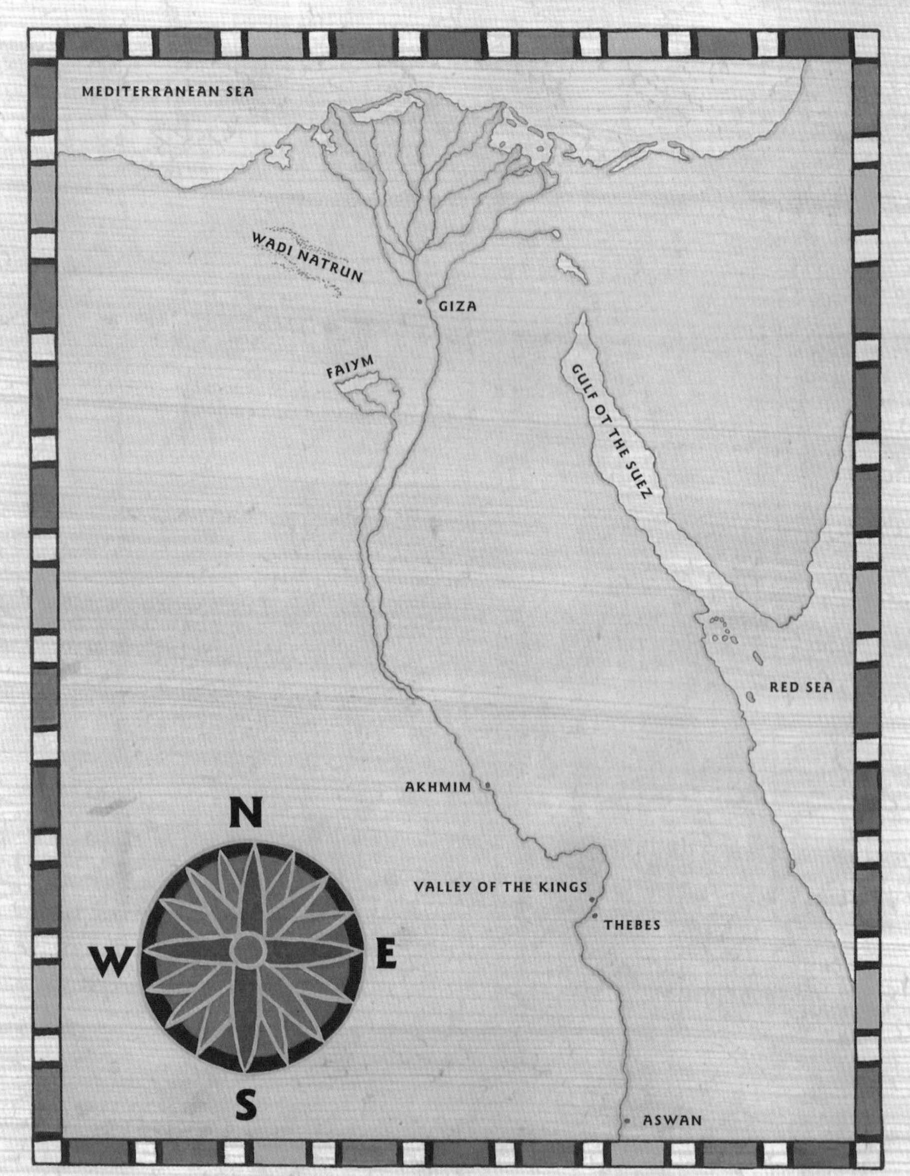


## A NOTE ABOUT THIS STORY

THOUGH WE do have some Egyptian documents on mummification, the ancient Egyptians never wrote down how they embalmed a mummy. One group of scrolls, called the Embalmer's Archive, from 50 BCE, tells us a lot about the daily affairs of the embalmer's business. We also have the Rhind Papyri from the Roman period of Egypt, which describe the rituals associated with embalming. Another pair of scrolls from the Roman period is called the Ritual of Embalming. But none of these scrolls tell us about the actual embalming methods themselves.

Most of the information we have on the techniques of embalming comes from Greek writers. Herodotus was a historian who lived in the fifth century BCE (484–ca. 425 BCE). He is known for writing *The Histories*, a collection of stories on different places and peoples he learned about through his travels. He described the mummification process. A hundred years later, Diodorus Siculus also wrote about how Egyptians made mummies, adding more details.

We have confirmed much of the accounts of Herodotus and Diodorus by examining the mummies themselves. Mummies have been x-rayed and more recently given CT scans.

Experimental work was done on mummifying animals by the Manchester Mummy Project in the 1970s and by Egyptologist Salima Ikram in the 1990s. In 1994, Egyptologist Bob Brier and anatomist Ronald Wade mummified a human body using ancient Egyptian techniques. This research has helped us to better understand the process of mummification.

Yuya and his wife Thuya are two of the most beautifully preserved mummies that we have recovered. Their tomb was discovered in 1905 by the American millionaire Theodore Davis and his team near the Valley of the Kings. Though it had been plundered in ancient times, it contained most of its original contents, so it was almost intact. This was before the discovery of King Tutankhamen, and the discovery of Yuya and Thuya's tomb made a sensation at the time.

Once the door to Yuya and Thuya's tomb was exposed police had to guard it day and night to prevent robbery. Arthur Weigall, the appointed chief inspector, made a camp over the mouth of the tomb where he slept for several nights, along with the artist Joseph Lindon

Smith and his wife, Corinna, in addition to the guards, whom perhaps they did not trust.

There was a small hole in the door, which showed that the tomb had been entered by robbers in ancient times. The excavators sent a young Egyptian boy through the hole to see what he could find. He returned with a few small things found in the shaftway, including a gold-covered scarab.

Davis called for Gaston Maspero, the director-general of the Cairo Museum, and he and Arthur Weigall joined Davis as the first door to the tomb was carefully removed. There was nothing more in the entry shaft. They took candles with them down the hall to the next door, which also had a robber's hole in it. The hole was small, so they took some of the stones away to make it larger. Even still, the portly Maspero became stuck in the hole, and Weigall and Davis had to push and pull to get him through!

The tomb was as dark as could be, and very hot. They could see the glimmering of gold from their candlelight. It took a moment for their eyes to adjust, and then they were dumbfounded—they stood there gaping and trembling for several moments. Here they were in a tomb that no one had entered for three thousand years! They went to the coffin to find the name of the tomb owner. Davis held the candles to the inscriptions so that Maspero could read them. In a moment he said, "Yuya," and Davis in his excitement moved the candles closer to the coffin. Maspero said, "Careful," pushing the candle away, as the coffin was very flammable. If it had caught fire, everything in the tomb would have burned rapidly, and they would have died.

They decided to leave then and come back with electric lights. The workmen took down the second door, and electricians brought wires and lights (there were no flashlights then). They held the lightbulbs over their heads and went back in. Every foot of the chamber sparkled with gilded furniture. In a corner stood a chariot, and there were three beautiful wooden armchairs decorated in gold, one with a perfectly preserved pillow. Lovely alabaster vases, filled with liquids. Boxes of fine workmanship. Yuya's sandals, placed as though for a long journey. Everything in such perfect condition it might have been placed there the day before. When Weigall saw the alabaster jar filled with liquid (which he thought was honey but was in fact natron), he felt faint from amazement.

When Davis entered the tomb for another look, he looked around for a minute and cried, "Oh my god!" and fainted from excitement. Weigall and Smith rushed to Davis's side and helped him to his feet, but he fainted a second time, it was so overwhelming to him.

The coffins had already been opened by robbers, and the mummies of Yuya and Thuya lay inside. Their faces so perfectly preserved, they looked as if they were sleeping and might awake at any moment. Their bandages had been torn off so that the robbers could steal their gold and jeweled amulets. But the mummy of Thuya had been carefully covered with a cloth; perhaps the robber had felt some shame to leave her exposed.

Davis wrote of Thuya: "I had occasion to sit by her in the tomb for nearly an hour, and having nothing else to do or see, I studied her face and indulged in speculations germane to the situation, until her dignity and character so impressed me that I almost found it necessary to apologize for my presence."

Yuya's second coffin was gilded in silver, and the sealed air of the tomb had kept it bright and shiny. Upon them removing the coffin to the air outside, it tarnished almost instantly to black.

When Corinna Smith, Lindon Smith's wife, first entered Yuya's tomb, the sight of it was too much for her altogether, and she burst into a crying fit so severe that she had to be taken out.

Arthur Weigall's wife, Hortense, wrote to him, describing how she reacted upon reading his letter about the discovery of Yuya and Thuya's tomb: "I felt like someone in a dream and I grew first cold and then hot as I read, and when the letter was finished my cheeks were so crimson that Mamma thought I had fever! . . . I don't wonder that people fainted and cried!"

Empress Eugenie, widow of Napoleon III of France, came to visit the tomb. She said to James Edward Quibell, "Do tell me something of the discovery of the tomb." Quibell replied: "With pleasure, but I regret that I cannot offer you a chair." The empress said, "Why there is a chair that will do for me nicely," and sat in a chair that had not been used in three thousand years! The archaeologist watched in horror, but the chair bore her weight.

Maspero offered Davis a portion of the find, but Davis felt that the contents of the tomb should stay together in the Cairo Museum, where they are today, along with the mummies of Yuya and Thuya.

Although Yuya and Thuya's tomb was spectacular, it was robbed not long after they were buried. The thieves took easily carried and exchangeable items such as jewelry, jars of oils, and linens and clothing. The excavators found the lids of the coffins opened and the mummies' wrappings torn to grab their amulets. The tomb was robbed a second time, probably when the nearby tombs of Ramses XI and a son of Ramses III were built.

Yuya's Book of the Dead is one of the best examples of funerary texts. The painted scenes are beautifully made, and the text is generally clear. It is only slightly damaged. Yuya's papyrus was written in a scribe's workshop with the spaces for the name of the deceased left blank. Upon the purchase of the scroll, Yuya's name was filled in. There were also blank spaces for personalized paintings of Yuya. In this scroll, Yuya is shown wearing a white wig, probably to show his advanced age when he died.

It is possible that Yuya was of Syrian origin, though we are not sure. The Egyptians had trouble spelling his name in hieroglyphs—there are several different spellings of his name on the objects in his tomb. Both Yuya's and Thuya's hair is yellow—it is unknown whether the color is natural or if it resulted from a reaction of henna to the embalming chemicals. It is believed that Yuya and Thuya were from the southern town of Akhmim, which would make it more likely that they were native Egyptians, though it's possible that Yuya's family was of foreign ancestry.

Queen Tiye was one of the most powerful queens of ancient Egypt. Her name appears beside her husband's almost everywhere, from large monuments to small jars. And, like her husband the king, Tiye was worshipped in her own right, most often as a personification of the goddess Hathor. Amenhotep III built a beautiful lake in her honor. She continued to exert influence in her son's court and may have been an influence in Akhenaten's religious convictions, though we do not know for sure.

On the next page is a chart of Yuya's family tree. There are a couple of people we are not sure about. It is not certain that Aye was Yuya's son, though some Egyptologists believe so. Nor do we know for sure whether Nefertiti was Aye's daughter.

## FURTHER READING


Aliki. *Mummies Made in Egypt*. New York: Thomas Y. Crowell, 1979.

Brier, Bob. *Ancient Egyptian Magic*. New York: William Morrow, 1980.

——. *Egyptian Mummies*. New York: William Morrow, 1994.

——. *The Encyclopedia of Mummies*. New York: Facts on File, 1998.

Brier, Bob, and Ronald Wade. *Surgical Procedures during Ancient Egyptian Mummification*. ZAS 126, 1999.

Brier, Bob, and Ronald Wade. *The Use of Natron in Human Mummification: A Modern Experiment*. ZAS 124, 1997.

Davis, Theodore M. *Tomb of Iouiya and Touiyou: with The Funeral Papyrus of Iouiya*. Bath, UK: Bath Press, 2000.

El Mahdy, Christine. *Mummies, Myth and Magic*. London: Thames & Hudson, 1989.

Fletcher, Joann. *Chronicle of a Pharaoh, the Intimate Life of Amenhotep III*. New York: Oxford University Press, 2000.

Harris, James E., and Kent R. Weeks. *X-Raying the Pharaohs*. New York: Charles Scribner's Sons, 1973.

Harris, James E., and Edward F. Wente. *An X-Ray Atlas of the Royal Mummies*. Chicago: University of Chicago Press, 1980.

Ikram, Salima. *Death and Burial in Ancient Egypt*. New York: Longman, 2003.

——. *Divine Creatures: Animal Mummies In Ancient Egypt*. Cairo: The American University in Cairo Press, 2005.

——. *Royal Mummies in the Egyptian Museum*. Cairo: American University in Cairo Press, 1997.

——. *Zoo for Eternity: Animal Mummies from the Cairo Museum*. Cairo: Supreme Council of Antiquities, 2004.

Ikram, Salima, and Aidan Dodson. *The Mummy in Ancient Egypt: Equipping the Dead for Eternity*. London: Thames & Hudson, 1998.

Leca, Ange-Pierre. *The Egyptian Way of Death*. New York: Doubleday & Company, 1981.

Pringle, Heather. *The Mummy Congress*. New York: Theia, 2001.

Quibell, James Edward. *Tomb of Yuaa and Thuiu*. Le Caire: Impr. de l'Institut français d'archéologie orientale, 1908.

Reeves, C. N. *Valley of the Kings: Decline of a Royal Necropolis*. London, New York: K. Paul International, 1990.

Reeves, C. N., and Richard Wilkinson. *The Complete Valley of the Kings*. London: Thames & Hudson, 1996.

Reeves, Nicholas. *Akhenaten, Egypt's False Prophet*. London, Thames & Hudson, 2001.

Winlock, Herbert Eustis. *The Materials Used at the Embalming of King Tut-'Ankh-Amun*. New York: Metropolitan Museum of Art, 1941.

# YUYA'S FAMILY TREE

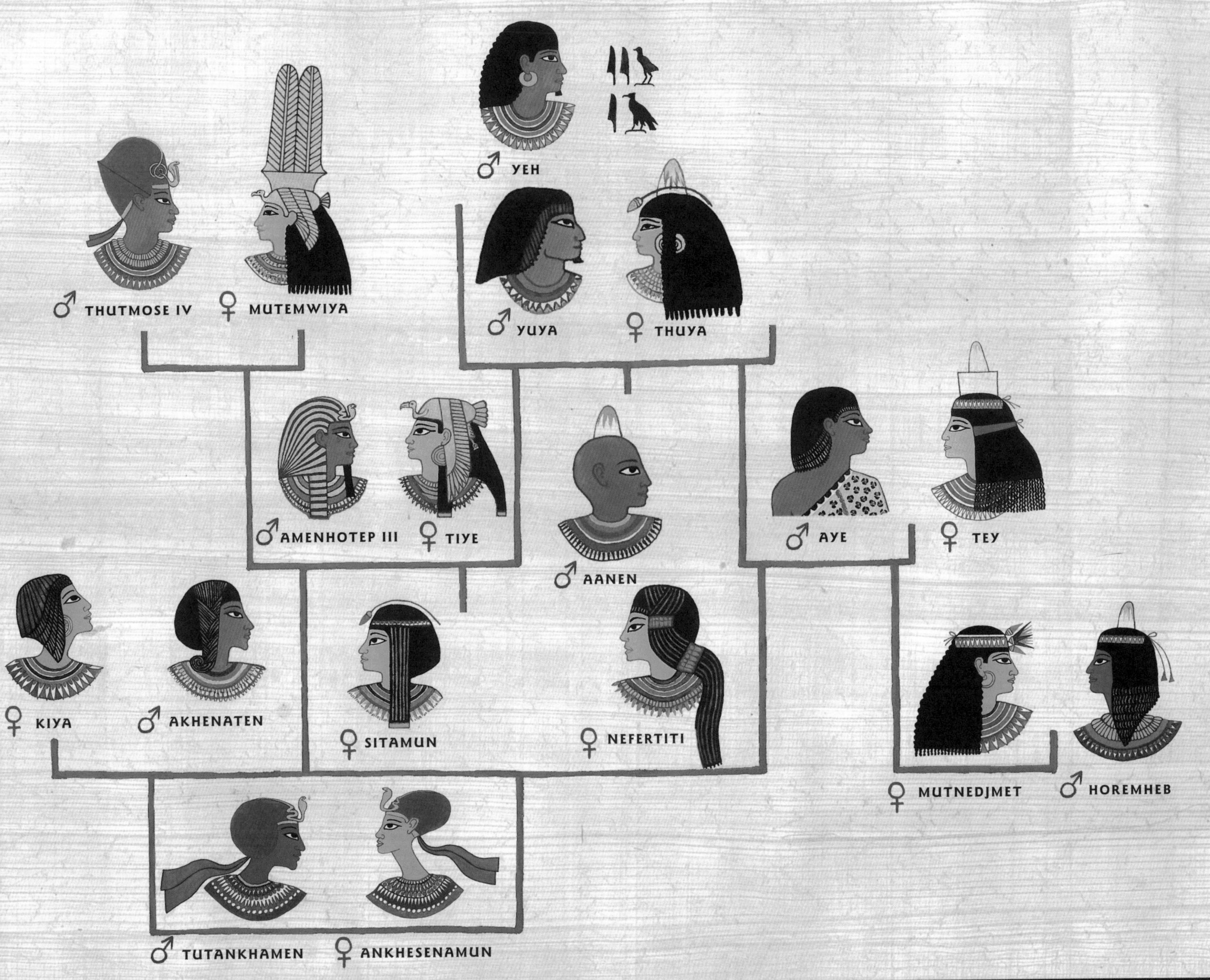

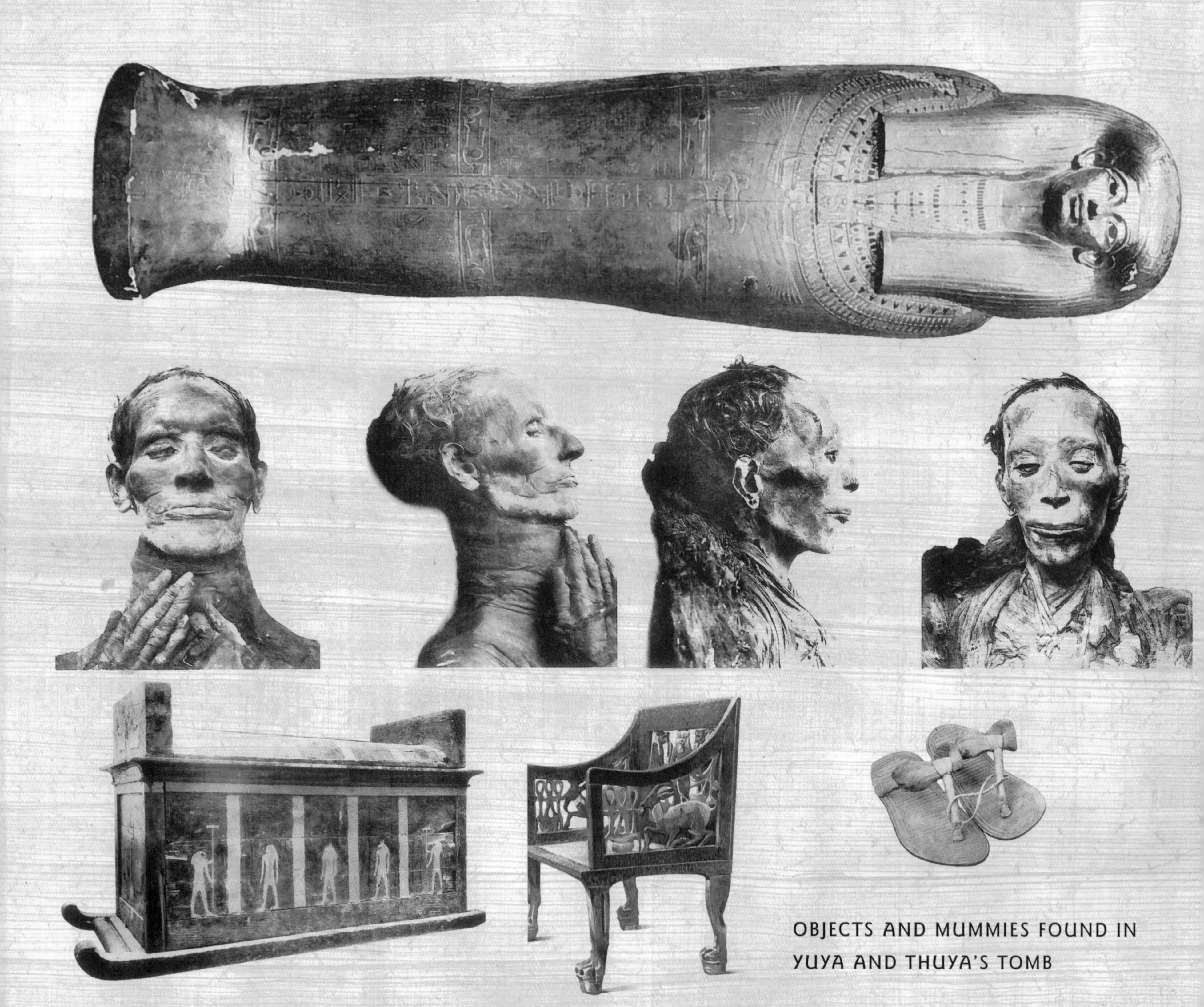

OBJECTS AND MUMMIES FOUND IN YUYA AND THUYA'S TOMB

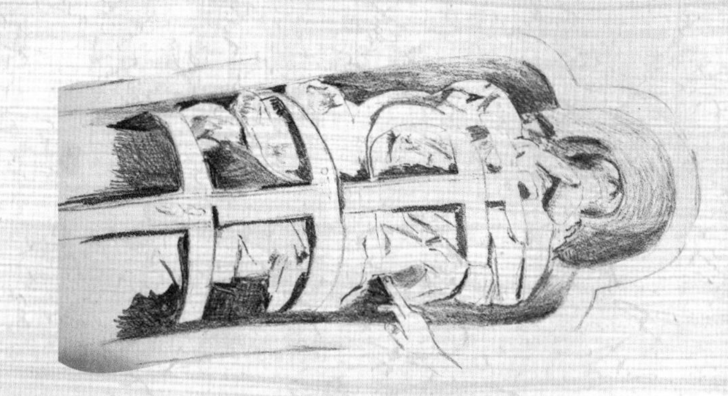

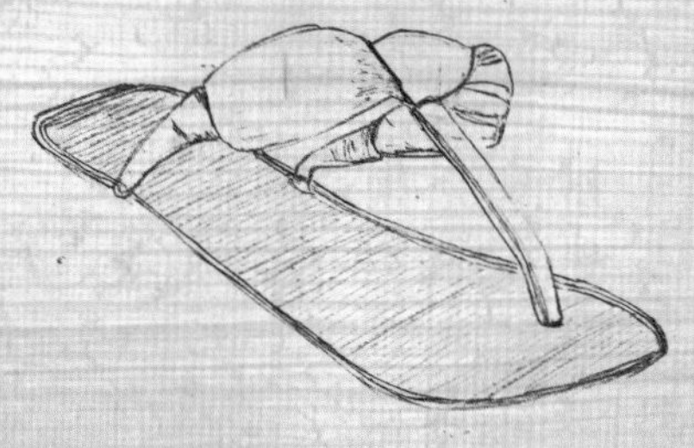

PRELIMINARY DRAWINGS BASED ON OBJECTS FOUND IN YUYA AND THUYA'S TOMB BY TAMARA BOWER

*Special thanks to*

**DR. BOB BRIER, DR. SALIMA IKRAM, TONY ASKIN, HALEY GOLD, HILARY ALLISON, AND SETH TOBOCMAN.**

*Hieroglyphic translations by*

**DR. MARY-ANN POULS WEGNER**

**Associate Professor of Egyptian Archaeology, Department of Near & Middle Eastern Civilizations, University of Toronto, Director, Toronto Abydos Votive Zone Project, Pennsylvania-Yale-Institute of Fine Arts Expedition to Abydos.**



**A TRIANGLE SQUARE BOOKS FOR YOUNG READERS FIRST EDITION**
**PUBLISHED BY SEVEN STORIES PRESS**

LIBRARY OF CONGRESS CATALOGING-IN-PUBLICATION DATA

Bower, Tamara. The mummy makers of Egypt / by Tamara Bower.

pages cm

"A Triangle Square books for young readers edition."

ISBN 978-1-60980-600-2 (hardcover)

1. Yuya—Tomb—Juvenile literature. 2. Mummies—Egypt--Juvenile literature.
3. Funeral rites and ceremonies—Egypt—Juvenile literature. 4. Embalming—Egypt—Juvenile literature.
5. Buria—Egypt—History—To 332 B.C.—Juvenile literature. 6. Tombs—Egypt—Juvenile literature.
7. Egypt—Civilization—To 332 B.C.—Juvenile literature.
I. Title.

DT62.M7B65 2015

932'.014—dc23

2015007488



ISBN ePub edition: 978-1-60980-601-9

Printed in Malaysia

9 8 7 6 5 4 3 2 1